OTHER CREEPIES FOR YOU TO ENJOY ARE:
The Ankle Grabber
Scare Yourself to Sleep
Jumble Joan

For Tom (RI)
For Herman (MK)

School Specialty
Children's Publishing

Text © 1988 Rose Impey
Illustrations © 1988 Moira Kemp
This edition designed by Douglas Martin.

This edition published in the United States of America in 2004 by
Gingham Dog Press
an imprint of School Specialty Children's Publishing,
a member of the School Specialty Family
8720 Orion Place, 2nd Floor, Columbus, OH 43240-2111

www.ChildrensSpecialty.com

This edition first published in the UK in 2003 by Mathew Price Limited.

ISBN 0-7696-3368-4
Printed in China.

1 2 3 4 5 6 7 8 9 10 MP 08 07 06 05 04

The Flat Man

By Rose Impey

Illustrated by Moira Kemp

Columbus, Ohio

At night, when it is dark
and I am in bed,
I hear strange noises.
They keep me awake.

Tap, tap, tap.
I know it is
the tree by my window,
blowing in the wind.
Its branches are tapping on the glass.
That is all it is.

But I like to pretend that
it is the Flat Man, trying to get in.
His long, bony fingers
tap on the glass.

"Let me in," he whispers softly.
Tap, tap, tap.
It is only a game.
I like scaring myself.

Rattle, rattle, rattle.
I know it is
a train going by.
It makes the whole house shake
and the windows rattle like
someone's teeth chattering.
That is all it is.

But I like to pretend that
it is the Flat Man, squeezing himself
through a crack in the window.

"You can't keep me out," he whispers.
Rattle, rattle, rattle.

Sshh, sshh, sshh.
I know it is
my baby brother,
making noises in his sleep.

But I like to pretend that
it is the Flat Man,
sliding around the room.
"I'm coming," he whispers.
Sshh, sshh, sshh.

The Flat Man clings to the wall and
keeps his back pressed against it.
His body looks like
stretched-out skin.
I know why.

I know the Flat Man's secret.
He's afraid of the light.
He hates open spaces.
That's why he creeps in corners
and drifts in the dark.

One flash of bright light,
and the Flat Man would shrivel up
like a crumpled sheet of paper.
One slight breeze, and he
would blow away.

So, the Flat Man slips and slides
in the shadows until
he is near my bed.
Then, he waits
patiently for his chance
to get me!

I do not hear a sound now.
I know that there
is no one there.
No one at all.

But I like to pretend that it is
the Flat Man, holding his breath.
He is waiting, not making a sound.

Then, when everything is quiet and still,
he will dart over to my bed
and slide into it.

Suddenly, I feel a chill
down my back.
I know that there is
a small crack near the floor,
where the wind blows in.
That is all it is.

But I like to pretend
it is the Flat Man,
coming closer
and closer.
He breathes his icy breath on me.
It makes me shiver.

I pull the covers up under my chin
and hold them tight.

I think to myself,
He is thin enough
to slide through a closed door.
He could creep into my room
right now.

He could be lying right beside me,
cold and flat.

I lie here, afraid to move.
An icy feeling is spreading
all the way through my body.

Something, or someone,
seems to be wrapping itself
around my chest.

I cannot breathe.
I try to think,
but my brain is racing inside my head.
There must be something I can do.
Suddenly, I remember
the Flat Man's secret!
He does not like open spaces.
He is afraid he would blow away.

I throw back the covers.
I flap them up and down
like a whirlwind.
"I will get rid of you!" I yell.
Flap, flap, flap.

The Flat Man flies across the room.
He tries to creep into a corner.

Next, I jump out of bed.
I point my flashlight at him.
"Take that!" I say.

I switch on the lamp.
"And that!"
I turn on the bedroom light.
"And that!"
Flash, flash, flash.

I can hear the Flat Man
cry out in pain.
He starts to shrivel up.
He curls at the edges
and floats towards the window.

I rush to get there first.
I throw it open.
He drifts out the window
and disappears into the black sky.

SLAM!
I close the window tightly.
Even the Flat Man could not get in.

"And don't come back!" I shout.
  I make a terrible face,
    just in case the Flat Man is looking back.

Suddenly, my bedroom door opens.

A deep voice says,
"What on earth are you doing?"

It is my dad.
He looks at me and
makes a face.
"For goodness sake,
close those curtains
and get into bed," he says.

I creep back into bed.
"I was just playing," I say.
"Playing?" asks Dad.
"Scaring myself."
"Scaring yourself?"
"It was only a game," I say.
"Hmmm," says Dad.
"You need to stop playing
and get some sleep."

Dad turns off the light.
He shuts the door
and goes downstairs.

Now, it is really quiet.
The room is dark.
I lie in bed.
I squint my eyes
and see shapes.

I see a big black dragon on the wall.
I know it is the kite
that my Grandpa brought me from China.
That is all it is.

But I like to pretend
it is the Flying Vampire,
ready to swoop down on me.
Wheeeeee!